# iHorror

STEVE BARLOW ✝ STEVE SKIDMORE

# WEREWOLF HUNTER

# iHorror

# WEREWOLF
# HUNTER

Steve Barlow
&
Steve Skidmore

Illustrated by
Paul Davidson

ORCHARD BOOKS

ORCHARD BOOKS
338 Euston Road, London NW1 3BH
Orchard Books Australia
Level 17/207 Kent St, Sydney, NSW 2000

A Paperback Original
First published in Great Britain in 2011

A CIP catalogue record for this book is available from
the British Library.

ISBN 978 1 40830 987 2

1 3 5 7 9 10 8 6 4 2

Printed in Great Britain

The paper and board used in this paperback are natural recyclable
products made from wood grown in sustainable forests. The
manufacturing processes conform to the environmental regulations of
the country of origin.

Orchard Books is a division of Hachette Children's Books,
an Hachette UK company

www.hachette.co.uk

# iHorror

"*You better watch out,
unless you want to die.*"

Victoria Boatwright

# iHorror

There is a dark, unseen world around us, of supernatural horrors beyond our imagination. Sometimes the worlds of humans and horrors collide, threatening our very existence.

In iHorror, you make decisions that will affect how the story unfolds. Each section of this book is numbered. At the end of most sections, you will have to make a choice. The choice you make will take you to a different section of the book.

Some of your choices will help you to complete the adventure successfully. But choose wisely. Make the wrong choice and you could wind up dead!

Dare you enter the world of iHorror?
Fight your fear. Choose your fate...

# Who is the Hunter?

You are the Hunter, protecting the world of humans from supernatural horrors in all their forms. Vampires, werewolves, demons, zombies – you have fought all these creatures and more, and you've always beaten them... so far.

Over more years than you can remember you have become an expert in martial arts, including Jujitsu, Wing Chun and Taekwondo. You have amassed a store of weapons for every occasion: from an ancient silver sword, passed down through generations of werewolf hunters; to powerful chemical stink bombs, which upset a werewolf's sense of smell, and lethal flame-throwing guns. Whatever it takes to defeat the creatures of the dark, you will use.

Prepare to face your latest test in *Werewolf Hunter*.

# And so it begins...

You have been contacted by Marty Boyd, director
of Timber International, a logging firm based in
Ontario, Canada. One of his logging crews – twelve
lumberjacks – went missing in the depths of the
Canadian forests a couple of days ago. It was what
happened to them that aroused your interest.

During an online conference with Marty, you find
out that all contact was lost with the crew for two
days. A search party was sent out to find them. It
found the mutilated body of one of the lumberjacks,
lying in thick snow near the logging camp. There was
no sign of the others. Around the dead body were a
mixture of human footprints and wolf paw prints.

This didn't really surprise you, as you know wolves
could have fed on the body after it was killed by
something else. What did surprise you was that Marty
said there were no wolf prints going towards the body
– only leading away from it. And they weren't normal
prints; they were supernaturally large. Marty even
emailed you a photo of them.

After studying the outlines in the snow – coloured
red by the dead lumberjack's blood – you knew Marty
was right to contact you. He has a serious werewolf
problem! You explained this to him, and he hired you
on the spot – whatever it takes, whatever the price.

You promised to get over to Canada straight away – and that's where you're heading now in your private jet. Your weapons and equipment are packed, but after looking at the size of the footprints again, you know it's going to take more than that this time. This mission could test your courage and fighting skills to the limit.

You fly off through the night towards your destiny with the creatures of the dark.

‡ *Go to 1.*

# 1

It is mid-afternoon by the time you land at a small airfield a few miles from the logging camp. A team of security men from Timber International meets you. Their leader, Chuck Bradfield, says that they will accompany you to the camp, which lies in the mountains to the north.

"Thanks," you reply, "but this is my mission. I don't want to be responsible for you becoming wolf meat."

Bradfield nods. "Rather you than me. I wouldn't want to end up like the guy we found at the camp. He was pretty chewed up by the time we found him."

A thought strikes you. "Where is the body now?"

"We brought it back here and put it in the equipment storeroom. We're waiting for a forensic pathologist to come and examine it."

You look surprised. "You brought it here?"

"We couldn't leave it out in the open. Who knows what kind of wild creatures would see it as dinner?"

"Or it might just see them as dinner," you murmur.

Bradfield looks puzzled. "What do you mean?"

"We're dealing with the supernatural, here – beyond natural. The laws of nature are there to be broken. The dinner can become the diner."

‡ *To take a look at the body, go to 29.*
‡ *To set off to the logging camp, go to 75.*

**2**

You reach into your bag and pull out your grenades.
One after another you prime them and throw them
into the pack of werewolves.

The first one explodes, sending a shower of deadly
silver shards ripping into the flesh of the werewolves.
More grenades detonate, filling the air with howls
of pain and anger. Several werewolves drop to the
ground, mortally wounded. Others panic wildly – your
sudden attack has caught the creatures by surprise.
Explosions light up the night as you toss more
grenades amongst them.

Some of the werewolves bound towards you,
but you calmly point your automatic gun at them
and take them down with a stream of deadly silver

bullets. They drop to the ground and begin their transformation back into human form.

Within a couple of minutes, you have laid waste to the beasts of the night. Only one of the creatures remains standing. You realise that it is Lykon. Blood seeps from a wound in his body, but the werewolf still remains proud and defiant. He stands staring at you with hatred in his eyes.

Despite the fact he is still in wolf form, he speaks to you. "Hunter," he snarls. "I underestimated you. You may have destroyed some of my wolfkind, but there are many more, waiting for my call. And I will speak to them. And you cannot stop me..."

‡ *If you wish to use a grenade to kill Lykon, go to 92.*
‡ *If you wish to shoot Lykon, go to 37.*

# 3

You veer off the track and into the forest. However, you quickly realise that you have made a very bad choice. The snow is thick and the trees grow closely together – driving the snowmobile and sled at speed is almost impossible. To add to your problems, the snowmobile's lights hardly penetrate into the blackness of the forest night.

You slow down and somehow manage to steer the vehicle between the trees, but you sense that your enemies are not far behind. Your heart races as you hear a great howl come from behind you. You are being hunted down!

   ‡ *If you wish to carry on driving in the forest, go to 36.*
   ‡ *If you want to try to get back onto the track, go to 78.*
   ‡ *If you decide to get ready to fight your foes, go to 32.*
   ‡ *If you wish to abandon the snowmobile and use your skis, go to 57.*

# 4

You stand by the door until the waitress returns. You ask for a table and she shows you to one near the kitchen entrance, before handing you a menu. She wanders away as you scan it – it is not one for a vegetarian! Smells of grilled meat waft through the restaurant reminding you of your recent fight in the forest.

The waitress comes back to take your order. You look up at her. "Actually, I'm really a kitchen inspector with the city's Health Department," you tell her. "I need to see that your kitchen conforms to standard."

She looks puzzled and emits a low growl. You see the hairs on her arms stand up. "Wait a minute, I'll see what the chef says." She heads back into the kitchen.

‡ *If you want to follow her, go to 35.*
‡ *If you want to wait for her to return, go to 66.*

# 5

You head towards one of the main wooden buildings. The snow is still falling and the cloud covers the sky, blocking out the moonlight.

Your senses are on red alert as you move across the compound towards one of the larger wooden buildings. You move carefully and quickly to the building and try the door. It opens. It is dark in the room, so you readjust your night-vision goggles and peer inside before entering. It is a scene of devastation; chairs and tables lie around, smashed into pieces. You see several large stains on the floor. You bend down to inspect them – it is instantly apparent that these are fresh bloodstains.

As you are kneeling over the stain, the door slams shut. You spin around, gun pointed and listen carefully. Is there something in the room? Your heart beats quickly as you stand up, peering into the darkness.

‡ *If you wish to move towards the door, go to 44.*
‡ *If you want to stay still and see if anything moves, go to 94.*

# 6

Sometime later you awaken. You stare at your body. It is covered in fur!

You sniff the air and lick your lips. Your long tongue lolls out and slavers across your enormous pointed jaws – you have the taste for blood!

You throw back your head and howl and howl in despair – you have become that which you wanted to kill – a werewolf!

‡ *If you are brave enough to begin your adventure again, go to 1.*

# 7

You radio air traffic control for permission to land.
They direct you to La Guardia airport. You fly towards
the airport as the console continues to beep – but
you realise that you aren't going to make it! You
desperately look around for a place to land but as you
do, the helicopter's rotors stop turning.

You try to control the stalled helicopter, but it is
hopeless – the helicopter plummets out of the sky,
taking you with it to oblivion.

⚑ *If you wish to begin again, go to 1.*

# 8

You see a pile of fallen tree trunks ahead of you. Legs
pumping, you head towards them as quickly as you
can – you know your life may well depend on getting
to them and trying to take cover.

You sense movement in the trees – the dark shapes
are keeping up with you and tracking your every move!

With a superhuman effort, you make it to the
logs, snap off your skis and leap over the pile. You
are breathing hard from the exertion and fear as you
check your gun, ready for whatever is out there...

⚑ *Go to 55.*

# 9

You kneel, take aim and fire. Flashes from the muzzle of your gun light up the night and the noise momentarily drowns out the roar of the Horseshoe Falls, which are just metres away.

The werewolf is cut down. With a howl it drops to the floor. You think your shots have finished the beast, but in the darkness it is difficult to be sure.

‡ *If you wish to go to the werewolf to check that it is dead, go to 49.*

‡ *If you want to shoot at it again, go to 39.*

# 10

You hurry back to your snowmobile to pick up your skis – you realise that you won't be able to drive the vehicle into the thick forest. You also pack up a bag with extra ammunition and one or two surprises for the werewolf, if you happen to meet it.

You make your way to the prints and begin to follow the trail into the forest. The snow is thick and it is hard going, but you know that you have to hunt down this werewolf if you are to complete your job. The cloud cover has lifted and you are glad for some moonlight, which helps you to see the tracks more clearly.

An hour passes and you are still following the tracks through the forest when suddenly the trail stops. Cursing your luck, you take off your night-vision goggles, light a flare and look up into the trees, hoping that the werewolf isn't waiting for you.

You see nothing, so you look around on the ground for another trail. After several minutes of hunting about, you come across a set of human footprints. You follow them.

Soon you arrive at a slope – you look down and see smoke rising above the treetops. You ski down the slope and come to a clearing where there is a log cabin with smoke coming from its chimney. There are lights on inside.

You take off your skis, load up your weapons and take out a chemical stink bomb from your bag. "OK," you mutter. "Here's Red Riding Hood visiting Granny – let's see what big teeth you have..."

&#8225; *To investigate outside the cabin, go to 84.*
&#8225; *To go straight in through the front door, go to 69.*

# 11

Before you can react, the creature leaps and smashes into you, sending you crashing to the ground. It pounces again and pins you down.

The creature opens its jaws – you can smell its putrid breath – it stinks of death. Its gorged tongue licks you and streams of spit dribble onto your cheek.

You try to fight it off, but you are helpless. It has you trapped. Its jaws open and snap shut on your neck. You scream in agony as, with one movement, it tears away a chunk of your flesh and swallows it.

The creature throws its head back and howls in triumph, before it returns to gorging on your body. You scream once more as the werewolf's deadly teeth open up your chest and it gorges on your heart.

‡ *You have paid the ultimate price. If you wish to begin your adventure again, go to 1*

# 12

Before you move down towards the gathering of werewolves, you break open some of your chemical stink bombs and cover yourself with the liquid. You don't want the creatures to be able to detect the presence of a human and you know that the chemicals will confuse their incredible sense of smell.

You have your gun ready as you move down towards the ice rink. Ahead, you can see that the werewolves have formed a circle around a huge man – this must be Lykon. He begins to speak in a booming voice.

"Tonight, my brothers and sisters, is our night! It is the night of the Great Hunt. The moon is full and our powers are strong. For thousands of years this land was the country of the wolf, home of the creatures of the forest and the night. Then humankind came and took it from us. It is time to claim back our freedom and take back what is rightfully ours. I will go to the human's symbol of liberty and send out our message of liberation for all our brothers and sisters. Bring the weak and helpless to me – and then we will kill them and bring them back to what they should be – creatures of the forests! Go into this city and kill as many humans as you can! The Great Hunt has begun!"

With that he turns into wolf form, throws back his head and howls. You have never heard anything like it – the sound of a hundred years of hatred, loathing, anger and frustration rolled into one.

It is a signal, and the werewolves respond. They instantly transform into wolf form, also throw back their heads and give off a great howling that fills the city. Lykon begins to move off and you realise that you have to act immediately.

‡ *To use your gun, go to 64.*
‡ *To attack using your grenades, go to 2.*

# 13

You pull back the throttle and drive towards the werewolf. But the creature has supernatural reactions – it avoids the snowmobile, leaping high into the air and landing on the snowmobile's sled.

Before you can spin around, the werewolf pounces and grabs you in a deadly embrace with its claws. As its fangs head towards your body, the snowmobile lurches sideways off the track and hits a tree.

The shock of the collision causes the werewolf to lose its grip on you. You take this opportunity to jump off the snowmobile with your gun ready.

‡ *If you want to shoot at the werewolf, go to 73.*
‡ *If you want to try to escape in the trees, go to 20.*

# 14

"Actually, I've got some work I need to do for myself," you tell Boyd. "Can I hire one of your helicopters to take me to Niagara Falls?"

"Heck, after what you've done for us, you can have the ride for free," he says.

You thank him and soon you have loaded the helicopter and are heading for the great falls that separate the USA and Canada.

With some quick internet checking, you find the address of Wolfiz and you land on the Canadian side of the border.

You hire a car and drive to the restaurant. It is just turning to dusk when you pull up outside Wolfiz, which is overlooks Horseshoe Falls.

Your load your gun and place your silver sword in its sheath hidden under your long leather overcoat. You open up your equipment case and take out a small syringe gun that holds a microchip tracking device. You also pick up a pair of special silver-based contact lenses. These silver lenses will help you to recognise a werewolf if it is in human form. You pop the lenses in and head into the restaurant...your old Scout leader always told you to "Be Prepared".

Although there are plenty of people eating in the restaurant, you are relieved to see that none of them are werewolves. The same cannot be said for the waitress going into the kitchen. Through your lenses, you see her for what she really is – a werewolf!

‡ *If you want to follow the waitress into the kitchen, go to 35.*
‡ *If you wish to wait and order a meal, go to 4.*

# 15

Whilst Bradfield prepares for the journey, you organise the burning of the bodies of the lumberjack and the guard in the camp's incinerator. You don't want them returning!

It is turning dark by the time Bradfield is ready and the pair of you set off on two snowmobiles with sleds full of equipment. Cloud cover stops any moonlight breaking through and the snowmobile's lights barely help you to see along the snowy track leading through the dense forest. You curse silently – this delay has not been good. You signal Bradfield to stop so that you can put on your night-vision goggles.

"I don't have any," Bradfield replies.

"I have a spare set," you tell him. You step off the snowmobile and move to your sled.

At that moment the cloud breaks to reveal a nearly full moon. At the same time the air is filled with a great howling noise.

You spin around – the howling came from nearby! Through your goggles, you see dozens of dark, menacing shapes moving between the trees.

You reach for your gun and shout at Bradfield to arm himself.

‡ *Go to 55.*

# 16

You quickly make your way back to your helicopter and are soon in the air following the werewolf's progress on your tracking screen. It is moving at speed and you guess that it must have transformed back into its wolf form. You know a werewolf can move faster than a normal wolf and has more stamina.

The creature soon crosses the river and heads into the American forests of New York State. You are pleased that you made the right choice – you would have lost the beast if you tried to follow it by car.

The route the creature takes confuses you – it zig-zags through the forests, briefly stopping in several locations before continuing south-east. You wonder if it is gathering together other werewolves – perhaps this is what the lumberjack werewolf meant when it mentioned the gathering of the pack.

You continue to follow the flashing red dot through the night. The werewolf is still travelling through forests and mountains, and still heading south-east.

As dawn breaks, you begin to suspect where the werewolf is heading – New York City! Your suspicions are confirmed as the moving red dot turns and heads in a southerly direction towards the George Washington Bridge. The pace that the werewolf is travelling at is much slower now, and you suspect that it must have turned back into human form.

You continue to monitor the movement. Soon the red dot flashes continually at one location. It doesn't move from this position for over thirty minutes. You check out the map and smile – the werewolf has stopped at Central Park's zoo!

‡ *If you want to land the helicopter, go to 76.*
‡ *If you wish to continue to track the werewolf in the helicopter, go to 81.*

# 17

Leaving the burning werewolf, you pull back on the throttle and speed towards the wall of flame. The snowmobile bursts through and you are soon moving through the forest, leaving your dead enemies behind.

You check your sat nav and head towards the logging camp. Although you have managed to dispose of several werewolves, you need to make sure that you have eliminated the whole pack – so you need to check the camp thoroughly.

You eventually arrive at the camp, without further incident. The compound is made up of several wooden huts. There is a great deal of heavy machinery and large trucks around, but there is no sign of life – living or undead. Although the camp is dark, you notice that there are pylons with floodlights surrounding the perimeter. You realise that there must be a generator around.

You load your backpack with equipment and ammunition, and attach your flamer and sword to your utility belt. You pick up your gun and head into the heart of the camp, scanning from side to side with your night-vision goggles.

‡ *If you want to explore the camp, go to 5.*
‡ *If you wish to find the generator, go to 87.*

# 18

You gesture to Bradfield and the guard to move towards the door as you keep a wary eye on the back of the storeroom.

But before they can move, there is an ear-splitting roar that fills the room. The crates fly through the air, hitting the guard and Bradfield. They crash to the floor, but you manage to dive out of the way. You look up and see a figure from your worst nightmare standing before you.

The figure is a hellish cross between a human and a wolf. Its body is horribly mutilated and it stands on its hindlegs, but it has human arms and hands, not paws. Its wolf-like face has chunks of flesh and fur missing, and the creature's internal organs hang from gaping wounds in its hairy torso.

Before you can react, the creature howls and leaps at lightning speed towards the guard. Its slavering jaws crunch into the man's neck. Blood spurts out from his jugular vein like a fountain and gushes over Bradfield's face. The creature turns to face you and crouches, ready to pounce. You have to act now!

‡ *To use your flame gun, go to 51.*

‡ *To use your handgun, go to 63.*

‡ *To try to get out of the storeroom, go to 11.*


# 19

This is no time to sleep, no matter how tired you feel. You head to the Central Park zoo, where the werewolf's tracking device is still registering. You pay the admission fee and go in.

You grab a coffee from the zoo café. The signal from the tracking device is coming from the Arctic Circle area where the polar bears are kept.

‡ *If you wish to check out the area from a distance through your binoculars, go to 97.*

‡ *If you wish to go to the Arctic Circle area immediately, go to 59.*

# 20

You run for your life! Legs pumping and heart racing, you try to get away. But within seconds the werewolf has recovered and it is soon right behind you.

It leaps onto your back, sending you crashing to the ground. Your weapon spins from your hand.

You struggle desperately to free yourself, but it is hopeless. You give a cry as the werewolf's jaws open and it plunges its teeth into the back of your neck. Your agony is mercifully short as with one quick movement, the werewolf snaps your neck.

‡ *Go to 6.*

# 21

You quickly plunge the syringe into the werewolf's back, deliver the microchip and spin away. At that moment the beast turns around and stares at you. There is hatred in its yellow eyes. Its jaws open revealing rows of deadly teeth. It pulls itself to its knees, hurls back its head and howls.

‡ *If you want to shoot the werewolf, go to 49.*
‡ *If you want to turn and run, go to 11.*
‡ *If you wish to get out your sword and talk to the creature, go to 62.*

# 22

You aim your gun, but before you can pull the trigger, the old man instantly transforms into a huge werewolf and leaps at you.

You manage to get a shot in, hitting the beast in the shoulder. The creature's fur flies and blood spurts out, but this doesn't stop it. It slashes at you with its huge paws, scissoring open your face with its sharp claws. You stagger back and shoot again. This time you hit the creature in the leg; it falls to the ground, but manages to clamp its jaws around your shin. You shoot again, but in its death throes, the werewolf crunches through your shinbone and tears off your lower leg from the knee joint.

You scream and shoot again. A hail of bullets tear into the creature's ugly head and it finally dies.

You are in extreme agony as blood pumps from your severed leg. You know you have to get help. You struggle across the floor to reach your bag.

You make it and fumble to get your satellite phone out. Frantically you press at the numbers, trying to get hold of Bradfield. It rings, but no one answers.

Sobbing, you reach for your med pack, but the pain is too much and you pass out never to awake.

‡ *You have failed. If you wish to start your adventure again, go to 1.*

# 23

You reach for your weapon, but the werewolf is too fast for you. It pounces, knocking your weapon from your hand.

You curse as the creature's claws slash at your face and cut deep into your cheek. Blood pours from the wounds, but you have no time to think about these as the werewolf once again attacks. It leaps and knocks you to the ground.

You struggle desperately, trying to fight off the werewolf, but the creature's weight pins you to the ground. You punch the werewolf on the nose – you feel its hot breath on your face.

The werewolf ignores your attacks and opens its great jaws, forcing its razor-sharp teeth closer and closer to your neck. You try to push its head away and then with one final effort, you try to break free, but it is hopeless. With a sickening snap, the werewolf's jaws clamp shut on your neck. You scream in agony, before your voice is cut off as the creature rips open your throat.

All you can see is a fountain of red as your lifeblood gushes out from your body, before you mercifully pass from this world.

✢ *Go to 6.*

# 24

You shoot at Lykon, but the werewolf is too fast for you. You have now lost the element of surprise. You rush to the window and stick your head out, trying to see where Lykon has gone.

Suddenly you feel a searing pain as the werewolf grabs hold of your head and with a supernatural force pulls you through the window. Your gun is ripped from your hand as Lykon stands on the statue's crown, holding you over the edge. The helicopters are now near and you can feel the wind of their rotors. Their searchlights illuminate the statue. You struggle desperately, but are helpless in Lykon's mighty grip.

"Hunter, thank you for coming – I will show my people what we can do to humankind. If the Hunter cannot defeat us, then who can?"

With that the werewolf throws you out into the dark night. Instinctively you flail at the air trying to grip onto something that is not there.

The werewolf howls a cry of victory as you plunge screaming down and down until you hit the ground with a force that shatters your body.

‡ *You have failed at the last hurdle. If you wish to begin again, go to 1.*

# 25

You spend the rest of the night listening for any movement or sound of werewolf activity from outside, but you hear nothing more – if there are werewolves they must be avoiding you. Dawn is breaking as the helicopter you asked Bradfield to send collects you from the cabin.

You return to the airfield via the logging camp to pick up your equipment and weapons. You inform Bradfield of what has happened and contact Marty Boyd to tell him that you have destroyed the pack that attacked the logging camp. You offer sympathy for the lumberjacks who had turned into werewolves and had to be killed.

Boyd thanks you for what you have done. "I'll transfer the money to your account today. I suppose you'll be heading home now," he says.

‡ *If you decide that your work is over, go to 88.*
‡ *If you want to head to Niagara Falls to investigate further, go to 14.*

# 26

You slip your ski poles back into your hand and head up the slope as quickly as you can, legs pumping up and down, trying to gain some grip for your skis in the deep snow. Your heart is racing as you sense movement behind you and among the trees to your side. Everything is a blur as you try to get away from your stalkers. You increase your speed and manage to get to the top of the slope. You are now on the flat and you thrust your ski poles into the ground to increase speed. A quick glance to the side confirms your fear – your hunters are still keeping up. You realise that you are never going to be able to outski whatever is chasing you.

⚡ *If you want to stop and fight, go to 55.*

⚡ *If you wish to find cover, go to 8.*

# 27

You move slowly towards the door, open it and walk out, gun held at the ready.

Suddenly you scream as you feel a searing pain in your arm. You look down in horror and your stomach lurches as you see a werewolf with your arm in its great jaws.

With a brutal tearing movement it jerks its head back and rips your arm from its socket before spitting it out. You scream in agony as you stare down at your mutilated arm and the hand, which still holds the gun. Blood spouts from the gaping wound in your body and you clutch at it with your remaining hand.

You are in total shock, and have no time to reach for another weapon. The werewolf pounces on you, knocking you to the floor and ripping at your belly to open it up and feed on you.

Your last sight is that of the great beast feasting on your insides.

‡ *You have paid the ultimate price. If you feel brave enough to begin again, go back to 1.*

# 28

You spin around and land a drop kick into the werewolf's chest. It staggers back and you follow up with a combination of punches that has the creature reeling. It pounces at you but you are ready – you fall to the ground, and using the werewolf's own motion, send it flying through the air and into a wall.

Before it can react, you take out your silver sword and thrust it into the creature's chest and through its cursed heart.

The creature gives out a howl that is answered by the animals of the zoo in a series of squawks and growls. Then it falls silent. Gradually, it begins to transform back into its human shape.

You search through the werewolf's pockets for any clues and pull out a brochure for the ice rink in Central Park. Written on it is a date – you realise that it is today's date and the word "Lykon".

You dispose of the body by throwing it into the polar bear's pool. "Extra rations," you growl, before heading off to the ice rink for your date with a werewolf...

    ‡ *Go to 41.*

# 29

"I'll take a look at the body before I head out," you say. "Give me a minute to get my guns."

"Why do you need guns to look at a dead man?" asks Bradfield.

"Sometimes the dead can be more dangerous than the living," you reply. Bradfield looks puzzled.

You return to your plane and arm yourself with your automatic handgun loaded with silver bullets and your flame gun – you know that you can never be too careful when dealing with creatures of the dark. Bradfield and another member of his team escort you across the camp to the storeroom. The guard unlocks the door, opens it and switches on the light. As you enter, Bradfield gives a gasp of surprise.

"What's the matter?" you ask.

"The body has gone," he replies. "It was on that table." He points to a wooden table. It is empty except for a torn and bloodstained body bag. Bradfield turns to the guard. "Who gave permission to move the body?" The guard shrugs.

You raise your handgun. "Maybe it moved itself."

You look down at the wooden floor and see several scratch marks leading away from the table. You put your finger to your lips and point with your gun towards a pile of crates marked "ANFO – AMMONIUM

NITRATE/FUEL OIL EXPLOSIVES" at the back of the storeroom. Is something hiding behind them?

- ‡ *If you wish to move towards the back of the storeroom, go to 89.*
- ‡ *If you wish to head out of the storeroom, go to 18.*
- ‡ *If you wish to shoot at the crates, go to 42.*

## 30

Still holding the sword at the creature's throat, you take your gun and aim at its head.

"I want you to back away now," you tell the werewolf. "And don't do anything silly. If you agree to go to Lykon and deliver my message, I will allow you to live... for now. If you don't agree..." You wave the gun in the creature's face. "Understand?"

"You are a fool," replies the werewolf, but nonetheless, it backs away, heading towards the Horseshoe Falls.

As it disappears from view, you check your smartphone to see that the tracking microchip you implanted under the creature's skin is working.

A red dot flickers on the map of the area and you smile. Your plan is working! Hopefully the werewolf will lead you to this Lykon and you will be able to deal with it.

‡ *If you want to track the werewolf by car, go to 47.*
‡ *If you want to track the werewolf using your helicopter, go to 16.*

## 31

With your gun and flamer in your hands, you rush outside. You feel a terrific blow to the side of your head and are sent sprawling to the ground. Your night-vision goggles fly off and your gun and flamer spin out of your hand. Stunned, you stare up and can just make out the figure of a werewolf standing over you. It howls in victory.

You can feel your silver sword in your belt and the chainsaw you dropped is lying next to you. Your mind races – you know you haven't time to try to reach your gun or flamer.

‡ *If you wish to use your silver sword, go to 65.*
‡ *If you want to try to use the chainsaw, go to 99.*

# 32

You leap off the snowmobile and arm yourself with your gun. You take up a defensive position behind the sled and prepare yourself for the arrival of your enemies, whatever they may be!

You do not have long to wait.

A pack of about a dozen supernaturally large, wolf-like creatures bound through the trees, baying and snarling. You know at once that these are werewolves!

They charge towards you and you take aim. A single shot to the heart of the first werewolf is successful – the creature falls to the floor, its blood blackens the white snow. The others immediately back off, snarling and howling. You peer out at your victim and watch it transform into human form.

Taking advantage of the break in the attack, you aim carefully, pull your trigger and despatch another creature. It also turns back into human shape. The rest of the pack throw their heads back and howl. Then, as one, they charge towards you. You manage to take out another creature with a bullet to its heart, but there are too many of them and the largest werewolf is just metres away.

‡ *If you want to shoot the werewolf, go to 73.*
‡ *If you decide to reach for your flamer to try to destroy all of your attackers with fire, go to 23.*

## 33

You feel that you are too tired to do without some sleep, so you head into Central Park and find a clump of bushes, not too far from the zoo.

You huddle under the bushes and set your tracking device to bleep if the werewolf moves. You also set your watch alarm for a couple of hours... Then you close your eyes for some well-earned rest.

✦ *Go to 45.*

## 34

As the werewolf completes its transformation, you aim your gun at the creature's heart and pull the trigger.

A hail of bullets hit its target and the werewolf drops to the floor. It throws back its head and howls as you pull your trigger once again. The howling is cut off.

Bradfield looks on in amazement as the werewolf returns to human form. Not you though, you have seen this type of thing far too many times for anything to amaze you any more.

You point at the lumberjack and the guard on the floor. "You will need to make sure that these bodies are burned."

"Why?" asks a puzzled Bradfield.

"To make sure they don't transform back into a werewolf."

"Is that possible?" he asks. "Aren't your silver bullets enough to have killed them?"

"Usually, but it always pays to be careful," you reply. "Burning the bodies or cutting off their heads with a silver sword just makes sure. Better safe than being bitten."

"Do you want to do it?" asks Bradfield.

You shake your head. "I don't have the time, I need to get up to that logging camp, before it turns dark."

"Then, do you want me to come with you?" asks Bradfield. "I can be ready in about an hour."

‡ *If you want to set off in an hour with Bradfield, go to 15.*

‡ *If you want to set off on your own immediately, go to 46.*

## 35

Gun ready under your coat, you swing open the kitchen door and storm in.

The waitress is shocked to see you charging in. A grizzled chef stands over a flaming griddle. "What the heck are you doing?" he growls.

Your lenses also reveal his true nature – you can see the outline of his wolf form. You glance around – there is no one else in the kitchen.

&#10013; *If you want to talk to them, go to 43.*
&#10013; *If you want to attack them, go to 83.*

## 36

With your enemies in hot pursuit, you twist the throttle hard. The snowmobile lurches forward catching you by surprise – heading straight towards a tree! Desperately you turn away, but you are too slow. The vehicle smashes into the tree and sends you flying. With a sickening thud your head hits the tree and you crash into the snow. Through blurred eyes, you see a huge wolf-like figure. It growls and smiles, showing its razor-sharp teeth. You try to stand, but you collapse back into the thick snow.

&#10013; *Go to 6.*

# 37

Before you can pull the trigger, Lykon bounds away at supernatural speed. You send a stream of bullets after the creature, but don't hit it. Within seconds it is out of sight.

You curse and wonder where it is going to deliver the message of "liberation". You recall his words, "I will go to the human's symbol of liberty", and it hits you – it's heading for the Statue of Liberty! But how could it deliver its message to the world from there? A werewolf on top of the Statue of Liberty! It would be a media sensation – TV stations would cover the story and send it all over the world! Within minutes it would be on every network, every internet video site! Lykon calling to all those hidden creatures of the night across the world, bidding them to come together and join the Great Hunt, not just across America, but throughout the world!

You have to get to the Statue of Liberty as fast as possible!

‡  *Go to 79.*

# 38

You pick up your gun and flamer, and head to the equipment store with Bradfield.

You enter and see an empty table. A guard is standing by it.

"Any ideas on where it's gone?" asks Bradfield.

The guard shrugs. "No one knows." He holds out a body bag, which has been ripped open. "We just found this. The body was in it."

"And isn't any more..." you mutter.

As you step forward to examine the body bag, you hear a noise coming from the back of the storeroom. You spin around and listen carefully.

"What was...?"

"Shhh!" You cut off Bradfield and put your finger to your lips. You point with your gun towards a pile of crates marked "ANFO - AMMONIUM NITRATE/FUEL OIL EXPLOSIVES".

You realise that whoever or whatever was making the noise, is behind the crates.

‡ *If you wish to move towards the back of the storeroom, go to 89.*
‡ *If you wish to head out of the storeroom, go to 18.*
‡ *If you wish to shoot at the crates, go to 42.*

# 39

You take aim again and pull the trigger. A stream of bullets finds its target and you know the creature is finished.

As you head over to the body, you realise that you have no information about the location of the werewolf rising to help you in your hunt. The trail stops here. You throw the werewolf's body into the river and watch it float to the edge of the falls and disappear into the watery maelstrom. You head back to the restaurant in the forlorn hope that you will find some information about Lykon. However, there are no more clues waiting for you, just a lot of cops wanting to ask you a lot of questions about how a chef burnt to death and the whereabouts of the missing waitress.

Eventually, they let you go and you fly back to the Canadian airfield to pick up your jet.

‡ *Go to 88.*

# 40

"Your arrogance is misplaced," says the werewolf.
In the blink of an eye, the creature transforms back
into its wolf form and leaps at you. You raise your
automatic gun and shoot. A hail of silver bullets cuts
through the air and hits the creature full in the chest.
It drops to the floor, twitching and yowling in pain.

There is a great howling noise and the rest of the
pack attack. You aim and fire, but the werewolves are
smart and spread out, coming at you from all sides.
You manage to pick off a couple more, but you realise
that there are too many werewolves to fight at the
same time.

‡ *If you wish to use your flamer, go to 48.*
‡ *If you want to head for the opening in the trees,
go to 36.*

# 41

You arrive at the rink to see a sign posted on the entrance.

## CLOSED
### FREEZING SYSTEM BROKEN. NO ICE!

"Not so cool," you think. You make for the top of a small hill, where you will be hidden by trees. Here you can wait and watch the ice rink.

Hours pass and it grows dark. Snowflakes begin to fall. The cold New York night means that there are no people about. You begin to think that this is a waste of time, and that Lykon and the Great Hunt is just a story made up by a group of crazy werewolves.

As the moon breaks out from the clouds, you see movement on the rink. Dozens of figures pour out of the shadows and onto the ice. "Funny," you think, "why would people come out onto a closed ice rink?"

You peer through your binoculars and, with your silver-coated lenses, you see them for what they are – werewolves!

‡ *If you wish to continue to spy on the werewolves, go to 71.*
‡ *If you wish to get nearer to the rink, go to 12.*

# 42

You shoot at the crates.

"What are you doing?" screams Bradfield. "They contain explosives!"

"Don't worry," you say. "ANFO isn't a sensitive explosive – the silver bullets won't cause it to detonate. These bullets will only affect certain things."

Bradfield sneers, "What sort of things?"

Before you can reply there is a howl and a creature from your worst nightmares staggers out from behind the crates. Standing before you is a cross between a human and a wolf. Its body is horribly mutilated and it stands on its hind legs, but it has human arms and hands, not paws. Its wolf-like face has chunks of flesh and fur missing, and the creature's internal organs hang from gaping wounds in its hairy torso.

"That sort of thing," you reply. Bradfield and the guard stand horror-struck. You shoot, but the wounded creature avoids your silver bullets, and pounces on the guard. It plunges its teeth into his neck and rips off a hunk of flesh. Blood smears the werewolf's jaws. Then the creature turns to face you and crouches, ready to leap and feast on your flesh!

‡ *To use your flame gun, go to 51.*

‡ *To shoot at the creature again, go to 63.*

‡ *To try to get out of the room, go to 11.*

# 43

"I'm from the city's Health Department," you reply. "I'm keeping the public safe from Lykon."

At the mention of the name, the chef and waitress look at each other, then, as one, they turn into their wolf form and pounce.

However, you are ready for them. You whip out your gun and let loose with a burst of silver bullets. They rip into the male werewolf and he flies back, crashing into the deep-fat fryer. The hot oil drenches the werewolf and it bursts into flames.

Heat from the flames causes you to shield your eyes, and the female werewolf takes her opportunity. She smashes into you and bounds out of the kitchen door. You leave the burning werewolf and follow the female beast through the restaurant, racing past the horrified customers.

"Pest control! Coming through," you shout at them, as you chase the werewolf out of the restaurant.

The creature is fast, and springs across the road, causing cars and bikes to screech to a halt. You dodge the vehicles and shoot at the creature. You hear a yowl and know that you've scored a hit. That should slow it down, you think.

Your suspicions are confirmed as you see the creature ahead of you, running alongside Niagara Parkway towards the Horseshoe Falls. You continue to give chase. Motorists honk their horns and swerve out of the path of both the werewolf and you.

The creature suddenly veers to the right, leaps over a fence and heads towards the edge of the Niagara River and the great falls. You follow the beast and soon have it in your sights.

    ✣ *If you want to shoot to kill, go to 9.*
    ✣ *If you want to shoot to wound, go to 95.*

# 44

You step slowly towards the door, looking around to see whatever may be in the room as your ears strain to hear any sign of movement.

Suddenly there is a roar to your right, you spin around and a huge figure of a werewolf leaps at you, knocking you to the floor. Your night-vision goggles fly off – you can see nothing in the pitch black!

You still have your gun and you fire blindly. Each shot briefly lights up the room and you catch glimpses of your attacker. You can see that its leg is blackened and burnt – this must have been one of the werewolves you left in the forest!

You feel a searing pain in your leg and realise that the werewolf's claw has ripped into your flesh. Again you shoot around in desperation. There is a yelp and

you know you have scored a hit, but is it a fatal one?

You pull the trigger again, but there is just a clicking noise – you have run out of bullets! Quickly, you crawl along the ground whilst reaching for your flamer. You know you are fighting for your life!

There is a searing pain in your shoulder. You cry out as the werewolf's teeth bite into your flesh. You manage to throw the creature away from your body, almost passing out in pain as your skin is torn away.

Despite the fact that you are bleeding badly, you still manage to pull the trigger of the flamer and light up the room. You recoil in horror as you see the werewolf standing over you. It throws back its head and howls in victory.

‡ *If you want to blast the werewolf with your flamer, go to 93.*

‡ *If you want to use your silver sword, go to 65.*

# 45

The tracking device bleeps and you awake with a jump. Your head is still fuzzy with sleep as you look around you.

You see that you are surrounded by a group of figures wearing hooded tracksuits. At first you cannot make out their faces underneath the hoods. You sit up and slowly move your hand towards your gun.

One of the figures takes down its hood – your heart skips a beat as you see that it is the female waitress from Wolfiz. As one, the others take down their hoods – your silver contact lenses reveal that they are all werewolves!

"Hello, Hunter," growls the werewolf waitress. "You should not have let me live!" She holds up the microchip. "Not a very nice thing to inject into my body. But Lykon guessed you may have done something like this, and he used the microchip to locate your tracer."

In an instant the others transform into their wolf forms. You leap up and throw a punch at the waitress werewolf. She staggers back.

‡ *To shoot the werewolf, go to 73.*
‡ *To try to escape by running away, go to 20.*

# 46

"It's getting dark," you tell Bradfield. "I want to get to the logging camp as soon as possible. And you need to make sure that the bodies of the guard and lumberjack are burned. You don't want them returning!"

You are soon ready and set off on your snowmobile. Your weapons and equipment are packed onto a sled attached to the snowmobile. You follow your sat nav and head north along the snowy forest tracks, towards the logging camp.

Time passes and darkness falls. Thick cloud cover stops any moonlight lighting up your way. The snowmobile's lights make little impression on the darkness, so you put on your infrared night-vision goggles to help you see better.

Heavy snow begins to fall, and soon the tracks and pine trees of the forest are further covered in a thick blanket. The snowmobile struggles to keep a grip on the ground. You look at your sat nav. The logging camp is still a mile away. You have alpine skis on the sled. What should you do?

‡ If you decide to ski to the camp, go to 67.
‡ If you want to continue on the snowmobile, go to 85.

# 47

You head back to your car and drive off, following the tracking device implanted in the werewolf. You soon realise that the creature must have turned back into its wolf form as it is moving south at high speed.

Time passes, and you continue to follow the red flickering dot. Suddenly, you let out a curse – the red dot is moving across the river towards the US side. The werewolf must be swimming across the water and there is no road bridge crossing for miles!

You step on the accelerator, but soon the red dot disappears from the range of your tracking device – you have lost its trail. You spend the next few hours driving around, desperately hoping to pick up the signal again, but the trail has gone cold – you have lost track of the werewolf.

There is nothing for you to do, but to return to the airfield in Canada and fly home...

‡ *Go to 88.*

# 48

You aim the flamer and pull the trigger. A sheet of flame spurts out across the clearing and sets fire to the trees. You twist the throttle to send the snowmobile surging forward and circle the clearing shooting at the trees and any werewolf that gets in your way.

Soon all the trees surrounding the clearing and the piles of tree trunks are burning. Several of the werewolves are on fire and the air is filled with the stench of burning fur. As you'd hoped, the werewolves are confused and disorientated.

You switch to your handgun and ride around the clearing. Any werewolf that gets near to you is quickly put down with a shot to the heart.

The fire is still burning fiercely and you realise that you will have to get out of the circle of flame. Leaving the remaining werewolves, you steer your snowmobile to the opening and pull back hard on the throttle.

As you speed towards your escape, a werewolf bounds alongside. You pick up your flamer and pull the trigger. A sheet of flame engulfs the beast's leg, but it is not dead.

‡ *If you want to finish off the creature, go to 93.*
‡ *If you want to escape from the flames go to 17.*


# 49

The werewolf springs and with a supernatural leap pounces on you. Your gun spins from your grip and you desperately try to reach for your sword.

**48:** You blast the werewolf's leg with your flamer.

Although wounded, the werewolf's grip is powerful, but you manage to twist, spin round and hold the beast in a headlock. It roars in defiance and with a movement of its shoulders, sends you flying over its hairy back. You land with a crunch on the ground and take the chance to unsheathe your sword and flip back up onto your feet. You hold out the sword. "Come on then, if you think you're big enough," you taunt.

The werewolf backs off and you advance. The creature has its back against a barrier stopping people from getting too near to the edge of the river and the Horseshoe Falls. You can feel the spray from the water as you get near the beast.

Suddenly the werewolf springs forward. You thrust with the sword and pierce through the creature's skin and bone, into its chest. However, the werewolf grabs hold of the sword and stumbles back, pulling you too. It tumbles over the barrier, taking you with it.

You both fall into the river, locked in each other's grip. The powerful current takes hold of you, sending you towards the falls. You both realise that this will only end one way – down.

The werewolf cries a death howl and you scream, as both of you plunge through the watery maelstrom to your death.

✜  *If you are brave enough to begin again, go to 1.*

# 50

You make sure that the werewolf is dead, by finishing it off with your silver sword, then you begin to look around the cabin for any clues as to what the "Great Hunt" and "Lykon" might refer to. You know that lycanthrope is another name for a werewolf, but have never heard of a particular werewolf named Lykon.

There is a chart on the wall with Niagara Falls circled and with the date of the new full moon. You check your watch and realise that this is only two days away. The full moon is when the werewolf's power is at its greatest. Whatever is being planned is going to happen very soon! Also pinned to the wall is a business card. You take it off the wall, read it and laugh. "You have got to be joking."

You look around, but there is nothing else to be found in the cabin that could help you in your investigation, so you use your smartphone to connect to your database back at your house.

There is nothing specific on anything, or anyone, called Lykon, but you read an article on clinical lycanthropy, a syndrome where someone thinks they are an animal.

"Great," you mutter, "I've got a delusional werewolf on my hands."

‡ *If you want to contact Bradfield to send a helicopter to collect you, go to 25.*

‡ *If you want to ski back to the logging camp, go to 60.*

# 51

Before the nightmare creature can pounce, you aim your flamer and pull the trigger. A river of flame shoots from the nozzle and engulfs the creature. It howls in agony as it burns.

However, the creature staggers around in pain and crashes into the crates containing the explosives. The crates break open and the explosives spill out. You suddenly realise that the flames can act as a detonator.

As you sprint for the door, there is a flash of light and a deafening explosion. You feel your body being ripped apart. Then there is nothing but blackness.

‡ *You have failed in your task. If you wish to begin again, return to 1.*

# 52

The werewolf leaps as you pull the snowmobile to the left. The creature wasn't expecting you to do that and it misses you. Taking your opportunity, you head off the track and into the forest, twisting and turning the snowmobile between the trees. Although you are going as fast as you dare, you can sense that the werewolf and its pack are not far behind.

You peer into the darkness and see a clearing to the right of you.

‡ *If you want to head to the clearing, go to 90.*
‡ *If you want to drive through the trees, go to 36.*

# 53

You don't want to let Lykon know you are here by shooting at him, so you let him climb through the window. You guess that he is going to stand on the statue's crown.

You give him a few seconds, then climb through the window, and with a great effort manage to pull yourself up onto the edge of the crown. But as you do, you drop your gun. It falls through the air. You curse at your clumsiness.

Lykon is standing with his back to you. The helicopters are hovering around the Statue of Liberty, their searchlights illuminating the crown.

Lykon's booming voice can still be heard above the noise of the rotor blades. "People of the world, know that your time is drawing to a close..."

You take out your silver sword and a grenade. You shout out, "I don't think so, Lykon! It's your time to die..."

Surprised, Lykon spins around and stares at you with deep loathing in his yellow bloodshot eyes.

‡ *If you wish to use your grenade, go to 92.*
‡ *If you wish to use your sword, go to 74.*

## 54

You decide that you can follow the paw prints later and head across towards another wooden hut.

Cautiously, you enter the hut, ready for anything that might be waiting for you. Although it is pitch black, your night-vision goggles allow you to see perfectly. You see several crates stacked up at the back of the hut. On the side of the crates are the words "ANFO - AMMONIUM NITRATE/FUEL OIL EXPLOSIVES".

You move further into the hut, and your heart misses a beat as you hear a mighty roar. Before you can recover your senses, a huge werewolf jumps out at you, lashing out with its razor-sharp claws. It catches your face and you spin backwards – your gun flying out of your hand. You feel the blood dripping out of the lacerations on your cheek, but have no time to worry about the pain as the werewolf returns to the attack.

‡ *If you wish to reach for your silver sword, go to 11.*
‡ *If you want to use your flamer, go to 51.*

## 55

As you raise your weapon, dozens of monstrous dark shapes rush out from between the trees, howling and baying for blood! They are huge and their eyes burn red with hatred – you are being attacked by werewolves!

You manage to fire a couple of shots, but don't score a hit. There are too many of the creatures for you to deal with. You are helpless as the pack leap on you, ripping at your body with their deadly teeth.

Desperately you try to fight them off, but they are too strong and there are too many. You are knocked to the ground as the werewolves begin to satisfy their bloodlust.

You scream in agony as your flesh is torn from your body. Then one of the demon beasts opens his great jaws and snaps them shut on your throat. The last sound you hear is the gurgle of your blood gushing from your veins.

✢ *You have failed in your mission. If you wish to try again, go to 1.*

## 56

You back away from the werewolf, keeping it in view. You decide to change weapons to keep the werewolf covered. You pull out your gun whilst slipping the sword back into its sheath.

As you do, the werewolf takes the opportunity to transform back into its wolf shape. It lets out a savage roar and advances on you.

⸘ *If you want to shoot it, go to 39.*

⸘ *If you want to wait and see what the werewolf will do, go to 49.*

## 57

You move quickly, knowing that your life depends on it. You pick up your gun and silver sword – you can come back for more supplies – your immediate problem is to get away from whatever is chasing you!

You clip on your skis, pick up your ski poles, readjust your night-vision goggles and set off.

The going is hard and you can hear howls coming from behind you and getting nearer, minute-by-minute. You see a slope ahead of you – your heart is pounding from your exertions, and so you stop briefly to grab a breather and take your gun from your utility belt. You look back into the darkness of the trees.

Your night-vision goggles help you to see the outline of several dark shapes heading towards you at speed!

   ‡ *If you want to continue to ski away, go to 26.*
   ‡ *If you want to find cover and get ready to fight whatever is out there, go to 8.*

# 58

You shoot at the creature, but it is too fast for you. With a supernatural speed it leaps on the guard and rips at his throat. Blood spurts across the room, covering Bradfield. The creature howls with bloodlust, before turning towards you and readying itself to pounce.

   ‡ *To take another shot at the creature, go to 63.*
   ‡ *To use your flamer, go to 93.*
   ‡ *To use your martial arts fighting skills, go to 11.*

# 59

Checking your tracking device, you move towards the source of its signal.

As you approach the Arctic Circle area, you are surprised to see that the signal seems to be coming from within the polar bear enclosure.

There are no visitors in this part of the zoo, so you ready your gun – just in case. You check the signal again – it is definitely coming from inside the polar bear enclosure. You head to the wall and look over at the polar bear swimming lazily in his pool. The signal is coming from under the water!

"Looking for me, Hunter?"

You spin around and give a gasp of horror – it is the waitress werewolf you have been following. Despite her still being in human form, with one lightning fast movement, she knocks your gun from your hand and points a knife at your throat.

"You shouldn't have let me live!" She points at the water. "The microchip is down there. Not a very nice thing to inject into my body. But Lykon guessed you would have done something like this. It was just a matter of waiting for you. The Hunter has been hunted down..." She steps back and laughs, which turns into a nightmarish howl as the waitress transforms into wolf form.

‡ *If you want to use your sword, go to 65.*
‡ *If you wish to fight the werewolf using your martial arts skills, go to 28.*

# 60

You collect your equipment together, head for the door, open it and recoil in shock. Standing before you is a pack of over twenty werewolves. They stare at you with their malevolent yellow eyes.

You reach for your flamer, but before you can use it, the pack pounce. You are overwhelmed – jaws snap at you and claws dig deep into your flesh – you are helpless as the werewolves' blood and spit mixes with yours.

You pass out and fall to the ground, surrounded by your enemies.

‡ *Go to 77.*

# 61

You pull back on the throttle and speed down the track – a quick look at the sat nav tells you that the logging camp is not far away.

As you race towards the camp, you glance to your right and your heart misses a beat – your attackers are clearly outlined in the trees – you are being chased down by pack of about a dozen supernaturally large, wolf-like creatures, baying and snarling. You have suspected this all along, but now your worst fears are confirmed – these are werewolves!

You loose off a couple of shots, but don't succeed in hitting any of the creatures. You glance behind you and see that the werewolves are getting nearer.

You turn back and give a cry of horror – on the track ahead of you is a huge werewolf, standing on its hind legs, with its great jaws open.

You have an instant to make your decision!

‡ *To drive at the beast, go to 13.*
‡ *To steer away from it, go to 52.*
‡ *To aim your gun and shoot at the creature, go to 11.*

# 62

You take out your sword and hold it to the werewolf's throat.

"I don't want to kill you," you tell the creature. "But if you make a move, I will plunge this sword into your neck. Now turn back into human form."

The creature snarls, but in seconds the waitress has transformed. You keep the sword at her throat.

"What do you want with me, human?" she snaps.

"I have a message for you to take to Lykon – tell him that the secret of his Great Hunt is out, so he should call it off."

The waitress werewolf laughs. "You know nothing. Tomorrow night the moon will be full and you will be powerless to stop the gathering of the pack. There is a bad moon rising for humankind. Lykon is the Great Wolf – he will grant all werewolves liberty."

Thanks for telling me the time, now all I need to do is know the place... you think, but don't let on. "Ruling the world isn't all it's cracked up to be," you say. "Just take the message to Lykon and tell him he will have to deal with me, first."

The werewolf laughs. "You cannot stop us..."

‡ *To end the conversation by moving away, go to 56.*
‡ *To make the werewolf move first, go to 30.*

# 63

You take aim and shoot. Fur and flesh fly as the creature is hit by a stream of silver bullets.

It drops to the floor, snarling and howling. It makes one final attempt to pounce at you, but a well-aimed shot to the creature's heart ends its cursed life. It changes back into the human body of the lumberjack.

Bradfield is shaking with terror. "Wha— what is it?" he stutters.

"It was a werewolf," you reply. "But it hadn't fully transformed from its human shape when we came into the store. You say you found the lumberjack's body in the snow?"

Bradfield nods.

"My guess is that the cold acted like a deep freeze. It must have slowed down the transformation process, then when you brought it into the store it began to heat up and the transformation continued."

Bradfield shakes his head disbelievingly. "I thought werewolves were just something from horror stories."

"Stories sometimes have a nasty habit of hiding the truth," you reply. You turn to the dead guard on the floor. "Not a very happy ending for him," you mutter.

‡ *If you want to head off to the logging camp immediately, go to 70.*

‡ *If you wish to examine the guard, go to 82.*

## 64

You leap out and begin to shoot at the werewolves. Your surprise attack kills several of the creatures. You try to spot Lykon, but he is lost in the melee of bodies as the werewolves turn towards you.

You continue to fire, but there are too many to take on. You reach into your bag for the grenades, but you are overwhelmed by the number of attacking werewolves. Your screams echo around the park as your flesh is ripped from your body and your blood spills onto the ground. Thankfully you pass out with the pain.

‡ *Go to 77.*

## 65

"Don't think I'm done for yet," you cry as you take a firm grip on your sword and thrust upwards into the chest of the werewolf as it leaps towards you.

Despite scoring a deadly hit on the werewolf, the creature's momentum causes it to fall on top of you, jaws apart. It burrows its teeth into your neck and in in a final act, rips open your throat.

You heave the dead creature off you and hold your hand to your neck, trying to stem the flow of blood. Your vision becomes blurred and you feel weak. You collapse onto your back and lie helplessly, gurgling and spluttering as your blood drains from your body as you pass into blackness.

‡ *Go to 6.*

# 66

You sit sipping a glass of water until the waitress finally returns.

She sniffs, before saying, "The chef says its okay. Follow me."

You thank her and follow her into the kitchen.

As the door shuts behind you, a searing pain slices through your arm and you scream out. You look down and see a meat cleaver stuck in your bicep! It is being held by a grizzled chef, but through your lenses you can make out what he really is – a werewolf!

Before you can react, the waitress and chef grab hold of you and press your face onto the flaming stove. You scream in the heat.

"Did you think you could fool us?" sneers the chef. "We could smell you a mile off! Guess what's cooking tonight?" he laughs. "You!" He brings down the cleaver onto your neck, cutting off your cries, forever.

‡ *If you wish to begin again, go to 1.*

# 67

You park up the snowmobile and unpack your alpine skis. You realise that you can't take all of your equipment or weapons, so you choose your silver sword and gun. You load a backpack with flares, ammunition and food supplies. You set the coordinates on your portable sat nav, readjust your night-vision goggles and set off.

You make your way slowly through the deep snow. The forest path becomes narrower and narrower, hemmed in by the tall, snow-covered pine trees. The going is tough, and you wonder whether you have made the right decision.

You glance to the side and think that you see a shape moving amongst the trees. You stop and peer into the forest. There are further movements, so you slip your ski pole straps over your wrists and take your gun from your utility belt.

At that moment the cloud breaks to reveal a near-full moon. At the same time, the air is filled with a great howling noise. Adrenalin surges through your body as you see more dark, menacing shapes moving among the trees.

‡ *If you want to ski away, go to 26.*
‡ *If you want to find cover and get ready to fight whatever is out there, go to 8.*

# 68

As the console continues to bleep its warning signal, you look around, desperately hoping to find a landing spot. You see a helipad on top of a skyscraper near to Central Park and head towards it, hoping that you have enough fuel in the tank to get you there.

You bring the helicopter over the landing pad and hover over it. As you begin to bring the helicopter down, the fuel runs out, cutting off the rotors. The helicopter drops from the sky and crashes onto the roof, ripping off the undercarriage.

Luckily you are unhurt and can step from the wreckage, shaken but not injured. You check your tracking device – the werewolf has still not moved. You pack a dozen grenades filled with razor-sharp shards of silver and your ammunition in a bag, attach your gun and sword to your utility belt under your long leather coat, and take the lift to the ground floor.

The crash has made you realise how exhausted you are – you haven't slept for two days and you know that tonight is the night of the full moon, when this Lykon creature will possibly emerge and the supposed Great Hunt will begin.

‡ *If you want to find somewhere to sleep, go to 33.*
‡ *If you wish to go to the zoo and check on the werewolf, go to 19.*

# 69

You head to the front door, but before you get there the door swings open. You hold out your gun, but standing before you is a bearded old man.

"Howdee, come on in," he says. "I heard you stumblin' around out there."

"My, what big ears you have," you say.

The man laughs. "You sound like Little Riding Hood!"

No, I'm the woodcutter, you think. You follow the old man inside and note that he is limping. You look down and see specks of fresh blood splattered on the wooden floor. "Have you hurt yourself?" you ask.

"Oh no," he replies. "Just a wound I picked up years ago felling trees. I used to be a lumberjack and I liked the forest, so I built my cabin here." The old man sits in a rocking chair by the fire. "I don't get many visitors round here, what brings you to these parts?"

"Just a bit of hunting," you reply.

"Strange time of night to be out hunting. What you hopin' to catch?"

"Wolves."

The old man cackles. "Nothin' like that here!"

"You think so?"

‡ *If you want to shoot the old man, go to 22.*
‡ *If you want to make sure that the old man is a werewolf, go to 91.*

# 70

You point at the lumberjack on the floor. "You need to make sure that the body is burned – to make sure it doesn't transform back into a werewolf."

"Is that possible?" he asks. "Aren't your silver bullets enough?"

"They should be, but it's best not to take chances when you're dealing with the supernatural." You slip your gun into your belt. "I need to get up to that logging camp. One thing is certain, there are going to be more of these creatures up there," you say. You turn towards the door.

At that moment, you hear a growling and snarling. You spin around and gasp. The guard has obviously been infected by the creature's bite and is transforming into a werewolf! In the blink of an eye, there is no longer a trace of the guard. Standing before you is a monstrous figure of a huge wolf!

‡ *To try to shoot the werewolf, go to 23.*
‡ *To use your flamer, go to 93.*
‡ *To try to escape from the room, go to 11.*

# 71

You stand up and watch the werewolves through your binoculars, and see the creatures move aside to let the figure of a man through the crowd.

You gasp – the man is gigantic! His face is covered with a huge beard and his hair falls to his shoulders. The werewolves seem to be bending down as if in awe of him. It must be Lykon, you think. You reach for your gun and wonder if you could get a fatal shot at the creature.

As you try to get the creature in your sights, you hear a sound behind you. You turn and cry out as you see a werewolf bounding towards you at incredible speed!

‡ *To shoot the werewolf, go to 55.*
‡ *To reach into your bag for a grenade, go to 11.*

# 72

You smash open the window with your gun and begin to climb inside. However, the window is small and you struggle to squeeze through.

"What the hells' bells do you think you're doin'?"

You look across the room to see an old bearded man heading your way. He is holding a shotgun.

Before you can answer he aims at you and fires both barrels. The shot hits you in the chest and you drop into the room. You stare at the blood pumping from your body.

"Mmmm. Feeding time..."

You look up in horror. The old man is transforming before your eyes into a werewolf. In an instant, it pounces and its great teeth nuzzle into your belly. You cry out in agony as it snaps its jaws back with your entrails hanging from its nightmare mouth.

You scream, but there is no one to help you.

*✝ You have failed. If you wish to try again, go to 1.*

# 73

The werewolf leaps as you pull your trigger. The silver bullet hits the creature in its chest. It howls in mortal agony, but even as it dies, the force of its leap sends it crashing into you. You stagger back and your gun

**72:** The old werewolf rips out your insides.

spins from your hand. The rest of the pack are just behind their leader and leap into the attack.

Unable to reach your weapon, you try to fight off the werewolves using your martial arts fighting skills. But these are no match for so many supernatural beasts. Their sharp teeth rip at you, taking chunks of flesh from your body. You are in agony as the creatures continue their savage attack, until thankfully one rips off your head.

‡ *You have failed. If you are brave enough to begin again, go back to 1.*

# 74

As Lykon leaps at you, you twist aside and plunge the sword into the werewolf's shoulder. He howls in pain – the silver burns at his skin.

Again he attacks, but you manage to avoid him and once again score a hit, this time on his leg. Lykon again howls as the silver weapon does its work.

The helicopters are buzzing around and you know that this is going to be beamed into the homes of millions – you have to defeat this creature and show the world who is boss!

Lykon attacks again but with more speed, which catches you by surprise. A swinging arm catches you

and you teeter on the edge of the statue's crown.

Somehow you manage to regain your balance, but in doing so, you fall on your back.

"Goodbye, Hunter," growls Lykon. "Your death will inspire my brothers and sisters to revolt against humankind." The werewolf opens its great jaws to reveal its deadly yellowing teeth.

‡ *If you wish to continue to use your sword, go to 65.*
‡ *If you wish to use your martial arts skills, go to 100.*
‡ *If you wish to throw a grenade, go to 92.*

**74:** Lykon fights you on top of the Statue of Liberty.

# 75

"I should head to the logging camp as soon as possible," you say. "That way I'll reach it before dark. I'd appreciate it if your men would help me unload my snowmobile and equipment from the plane."

"Glad to help out," replies Bradfield. You head back to the plane with Bradfield and some guards to begin unloading your weapons and equipment.

You are nearly finished when Bradfield receives a message on his radio. As he listens, his eyes widen and lips tighten. He signs off.

"What's the problem?" you ask.

Bradfield looks shocked. "One of my men went into the equipment store. He says the lumberjack's body has gone! Who would want to take a dead body?"

‡ *If you want to send Bradfield to investigate the disappearance, go to 98.*

‡ *If you want to go to the equipment store to investigate, go to 38.*

# 76

You radio New York traffic control to let them know who you are, and receive permission to land on a helipad on the roof of a skyscraper that is overlooking Central Park.

You touchdown and check your tracking device – the werewolf has still not moved. You pack your equipment and ammunition in a bag and attach your gun and sword to your utility belt under your long leather coat and take the lift to the ground floor.

You have not slept for two days and are incredibly tired. You know that tonight is the night of the full moon, when this Lykon creature will possibly emerge and the supposed Great Hunt will begin.

‡ *If you want to find somewhere to sleep, go to 33.*
‡ *If you wish to go to the zoo and check on the werewolf, go to 19.*

## 77

Hours later you wake up. You open your eyes to see the huge figure of a werewolf standing before you.

It begins to howl and you realise that you understand what it is saying. "I am Lykon, your leader. You are now one of us – you will help to take back this world from the humans and feast on their flesh."

You lick your lips – this sounds good, for you have become that which you wanted to destroy – a werewolf! You throw back your head and howl.

*✢ You have failed in your mission. If you are brave enough to begin again, go to 1.*

## 78

You turn the snowmobile back towards the track and twist the throttle hard. Thankfully, the tracks grip on the thick snow and the vehicle lurches forward.

However, you are still being pursued – you hear the howls of your enemies at your back. You steer the snowmobile through the trees, knowing that any mistake could cost you your life. Your heart races as you twist and turn through the trees, your night-vision goggles helping you see in the dark. All the time you sense that your pursuers are gaining on you – their howls fill the forest air.

It seems a lifetime before you finally see the track ahead of you. With a cry of joy you pull back the throttle and guide the snowmobile onto the open forest track. You glance back and see more dark shapes moving quickly through the trees – your enemies have caught up with you!

&#8225; *If you wish to continue to drive along the track, go to 61.*

&#8225; *If you decide to get ready to fight your foes, go to 32.*

# 79

You head towards the nearest exit of Central Park and see a taxi driver standing next to his cab, eating a burger. You dive into the driver's seat, and ignoring the taxi driver's protests, slam it into gear and speed off in a cloud of burning tyre rubber.

You drive like a maniac through the crowded streets towards Lower Manhattan, running red lights and just managing to avoid multiple crashes. Police sirens wail in the distance, but you have no time for them – you have to get to the statue!

After a hair-raising drive, you reach the ferry port where the boats head over to Liberty Island. You leave the taxi and rush to the waterfront. Luckily there

is a motorboat tied up at the quayside. After a few
moments, you manage to start the engine and are
soon racing across the dark waters towards Liberty
Island. The full moon lights up the sky as you land the
boat on the island and race towards the base of the
Statue of Liberty.

The door to the statue is open and a guard lies
dead on the ground; a bloody lacerated mess. Lykon
is here! You head to the lift and take it as far as it

goes. Then you race up the many steps to the Crown Observation Deck.

You arrive, breathing hard, just to hear the noise of glass breaking. You rush around the observation deck and see Lykon climbing through a shattered window. You realise that he doesn't know you are here. In the distance you can see helicopters with searchlights heading towards the statue – you wonder if Lykon has informed the TV stations about his presence... You have to stop him delivering his message!

‡ *If you want to follow him through the window, go to 53.*
‡ *If you want to shoot at him, go to 24.*

# 80

You move slowly towards the door and open it. Before you step outside, you send a sheet of flame blasting out into the night. You see and hear nothing, so you step out and look around cautiously. Nothing is moving – you breathe a sigh of relief.

Looking down, you see a set of huge paw prints in the snow – they weren't there before! Whatever was waiting for you has gone – and you have a good idea what sort of beast it was!

You follow the paw prints. They lead to the perimeter of the camp, before going into the forest.

‡ *If you wish to continue to follow the werewolf's footprints, go to 10.*
‡ *If you wish to explore the camp further, go to 54.*

# 81

The red dot is still not moving as you hover above Central Park. A loud electronic beep sounds from a dial on the helicopter's controls – you have no fuel! You have only minutes of flying time left!

‡ *To try to land the helicopter in Central Park, go to 68.*
‡ *If you decide to try to make it to the nearest airport, go to 7.*

# 82

You move over towards the guard. Blood covers the floor. Bradfield looks as white as the snow outside. You reach down and examine the body.

"He's still breathing," you say. "That's a pity."

Bradfield is astonished. "A pity that he's breathing?" he shouts. "If he's alive, we need to get help!"

"No, he's dead, but his body is still alive..."

"I don't understand," replies Bradfield.

"It means that he's going to change. He's been bitten by a werewolf, his blood is infected. He's cursed – we need to act quickly."

"I thought it was moonlight that caused people to turn into werewolves?" says Bradfield.

You laugh. "I wish it were that simple. Moonlight can make them powerful, and werewolves are at their most powerful at full moon. But other things can cause them to change from human form to that of a wolf. Stress, anger, joy – anything that can trigger a chemical reaction—"

You stop your explanation as the guard suddenly sits up. Bradfield lets out a cry as the guard begins to change into a werewolf before your eyes! You have to act quickly before the transformation is complete!

⚐ *If you want use your gun, go to 34.*
⚐ *If you want to use your flamer, go to 93.*

# 83

As you pull out your gun, the two creatures instantly turn into their wolf form and leap at you, their great jaws open to reveal their yellow razor-sharp teeth.

But you are ready – a quick shot to the werewolf waitress's head accounts for one of the beasts and in the same movement you pick up a pan of hot oil, which you throw at the werewolf chef.

The hot oil covers the werewolf and it howls in pain. With a high kick to its chest you send it crashing onto the flaming stove. The creature ignites and you finish it off with a shot into its heart.

Eventually, the flames die out, leaving the werewolf lying smouldering on the grill.

Just how I like my werewolf – well done, you think to yourself. You look around the kitchen for any clues as to who, or what, Lykon is and what the Great Hunt signifies, but cannot find anything. With a growing sense of defeat, you head back into the restaurant. "Steaks are off tonight," you tell the customers.

You search around the restaurant, but cannot find anything that will help you. You realise that you have drawn a blank and have nothing else to go on. You return to your car, head back to your helicopter and fly back to the airfield to pick up your jet.

† *Go to 88.*

# 84

You move silently around to the back of the cabin. There is no back door, so you move to a small window. The curtains are drawn and you can only see the shadow of what you think is a man. You load up your weapons and take out a chemical stink bomb.

⁂ *If you want break the window and climb into the room, go to 72.*

⁂ *If you want to go back to the front door, go to 69.*

# 85

You decide against skiing to the logging camp – you don't want to be caught out in the open on skis and you wouldn't be able to carry much equipment.

You pull back the throttle on the snowmobile and carry on towards the camp.

As you battle through the snow, you see movement between the trees. The cloud breaks to reveal a near-full moon. You look into the forest again and see several dark, huge wolf-like shapes moving stealthily among the trees. You are being stalked!

⁂ *If you want to throttle up the snowmobile and try and get to the logging camp, go to 96.*

⁂ *If you want to stand your ground and fight, go to 55.*

# 86

As the werewolf completes its transformation, you hold up your hands in surrender. "Take me to your leader," you say.

The werewolf stands before you and opens its great jaws to reveal a mouth filled with pointed teeth. Your blood turns cold as you suddenly realise what it meant when it said, "But not as you are..."

Before you can react, the nightmarish creature pounces on you and its jaws snap around your neck. You try to scream but your cries are cut off.

The werewolf howls in victory and the animals join in, screeching, squawking, bellowing and growling as if in answer to the werewolf's cries.

You slump to the ground and pass out.

‡ *Go to 77.*

# 87

You move further into the camp looking for the generator. You move carefully, looking out for any sign of werewolf activity. Several of the buildings have broken doors and windows, and spilled oil drums litter the ground. You have no doubt that this was the scene of a fight – one that the lumberjacks lost.

As you explore the camp further, you see a sign for the generator. You head towards it and nearly trip over a chainsaw lying on the ground. You kneel down and examine it. There are the remains of dried blood on it. The snow about the chainsaw is also stained with blood and fur. "They tried to fight back then," you mutter. You pick up the chainsaw and head over to the generator shed.

The door is stiff, so you drop the chainsaw and push against it with your shoulder. It gives way. You step inside and curse – the generator has been smashed – there's no way you will be able to mend it. As you are examining the broken machinery you hear a noise outside.

‡ *If you want to rush out of the shed, go to 31.*
‡ *If you want to be more cautious, go to 80.*

# 88

You fly home in your jet, putting it on autopilot so that you can get some well-earned rest.

Arriving back at your mansion, you flick on the television to catch up with the news. What you see and hear horrifies you – a pack of five hundred werewolves has overrun New York City. Thousands of people have been killed and infected with the blood of the werewolf. You know that these people will also turn into werewolves and once they have taken over New York, who knows where the blood of the werewolf will spread? You had the chance to stop the Great Hunt, but now the world is doomed and there is nothing you can do now.

⚜ *If you wish to begin your adventure again, go to 1.*

# 89

You gesture to Bradfield and the guard to stay still. You ready your gun and move further into the storeroom one step at a time, listening for any noise.

You hear a rasping, breathing noise coming from behind the crates. You signal to Bradfield that someone or something is hiding behind the crates. Your heart races as you take another step forward.

Suddenly a creature from your worst nightmares

bursts out from behind the crates. It is a cross between a human and a wolf. Its body is horribly mutilated and it stands on its hind legs, but it has human arms and hands, not paws. Its wolf-like face has chunks of flesh and fur missing and the creature's internal organs hang from gaping wounds in its hairy torso.

It throws back its head and emits a deafening howl from its great jaws.

‡ *To shoot the creature, go to 58.*
‡ *To use your flamer, go to 51.*
‡ *To get out of the room, go to 11.*

# 90

You throttle back and burst into the clearing. You look and see many burnt tree stumps sticking out of the snowy ground. Piles of felled tree trunks lie around. Ahead of you is an opening in the trees.

You hear the howls of your pursuers and you swing your snowmobile around, pick up your gun and your flamer and turn to face your enemies.

At that moment the cloud cover breaks to reveal a near-full moon. The moonlight shines down, bathing the clearing with white light, causing your night-vision goggles to flare and momentarily blind you. A great howling fills the forest night.

When your vision is restored, you see about a dozen werewolves standing thirty metres away. Some are on all fours, some are raised up on their hind legs. All of them are huge and savage looking.

As the largest of the pack steps forward, you are amazed to see it transform into its human form. It stares at you and laughs.

"So you are the Hunter that our brothers and sisters of the dark fear so greatly?" snarls the creature.

"Well there's no one else here, so I must be," you reply. "And they are right to fear me."

The werewolf laughs. "There is no escape, Hunter. Accept your fate. There are too many of us. You are trapped."

You shake your head. "Not me, but you..."

‡ *If you wish to use your flamer, go to 48.*
‡ *If you want to use your gun, go to 40.*

# 91

"Have you seen anything unusual in the past few days?" you ask the old-timer as you reach into your pocket for a chemical stink bomb.

He shakes his head. "Not to my reckonin'."

"Well, maybe you hadn't reckoned on this!" you say as you throw the stink bomb onto the floor. The capsule smashes and a terrible smell fills the room. You are more than interested in the reaction it has on the old man.

He suddenly cries out in pain and squirms in his

chair, holding his nose and hollering and shouting, "Get rid of the smell."

You smile – you know that werewolves have an overly sensitive sense of smell – your suspicions that this is a werewolf are confirmed as it transforms into its wolf form. The powerful chemical incapacitates the werewolf and it rolls on the ground, yelping in pain.

"My, my, what a big nose you have," you quip. You aim your gun and pull the trigger. The bullets stream into the creature's body and it stops moving.

The creature turns back into its human form and its eyes flicker open. "You have won this battle, Hunter, but the war is not over," it sneers. "The Great Hunt is under way and you can't stop it. Our leader, Lykon, has called for his pack to gather and take back what is rightfully ours. You can do nothing..."

"I'm not afraid of the Big Bad Wolf."

"He'll more than blow your house down. Wait and see..." And with these words of warning, the werewolf dies. All at once the air is filled with howling that echoes through the mountains.

You wonder what the werewolf meant by Lykon calling his pack together for the Great Hunt – this job has suddenly taken a turn for the worse.

‡ *To leave and head back to the airfield, go to 60.*
‡ *To explore the cabin for any clues, go to 50.*

# 92

As you pull the pin on the grenade, Lykon attacks.
Before you can throw the deadly weapon, the
werewolf's jaws clamp shut on your throwing arm.
With a twist of its mighty head, it rips your arm from
its socket.

You scream in agony, but it is short lived. The
grenade is still in your dismembered hand and
explodes with a terrible noise, sending deadly shards
of silver out and ripping both your body and Lykon's
into shreds.

꙳ *You have defeated Lykon, but have paid the ultimate
price. To begin your adventure again, go to 1.*

# 93

You blast the creature with a sheet of flame. It howls
in agony and staggers about. The stench of burning
fur and flesh fills the air.

You blast it again, but the creature leaps towards
you, knocking you to the ground and crashing down
on top of you. Fire engulfs you, turning you into a
blazing human torch.

The creature throws back its flaming head and
howls as its skin blackens and begins to peel off. You
too feel your skin swelling as your body fluids swell

with the heat. You scream as the pain grows and your skin bursts open.

Mercifully, you pass out as you and your foe burn together.

‡ *You have paid the ultimate price. If you are brave enough to begin again, go to 1.*

# 94

You stand still, peering into the room and straining to hear any noise or movement. Seconds pass, but the only sound you hear is your heart beating quickly.

You continue to wait, staring into the room – waiting for whatever may be heading your way. Your breathing becomes shallower and faster.

Eventually you realise that it was either the wind that blew the door shut, or if something did shut it, then it must be outside.

You will have to head out of the room, but which weapon will you get ready to use?

‡ *If you want to use the flamer, go to 80.*
‡ *If you want to use your gun, go to 27.*

## 95

You take careful aim at the werewolf's hind leg. Despite the growing gloom, your sharpshooting is excellent – the werewolf falls to the ground, wounded.

You pull the syringe with the microchip from your pocket and race towards the creature. It is rolling around the floor in pain with its back to you. You point your gun at the creature. You can't be too careful – you know that a deadly beast is more dangerous when it is injured.

‡ *To use your syringe on the creature, go to 21.*
‡ *If you wish to put some more bullets into the creature first, go to 11.*

## 96

You open up the throttle and give a sigh of relief as the vehicle's tracks gain a grip on the newly fallen snow, and you set off at full speed along the forest track. Snow flies into your goggles, nearly blinding you – you can hardly see the track!

As you hurtle along, you glance to the side to see the dark shapes moving at speed among the trees. They are keeping up with you!

You reach down for your gun and fire one-handed into the darkness of the forest. You hear one or two yowls of pain – but you realise that there are too many enemies for you defeat by trying to shoot at them whilst driving.

    ‡ *To try to lose your enemies in the forest, go to 3.*
    ‡ *To carry on along the track, go to 61.*
    ‡ *To get ready to take on your pursuers, go to 32.*

# 97

You head out of the café and find a place from which to observe the Arctic Circle enclosure.

You take out your binoculars and scan the area. You are surprised to see that there is no one around. You check the transmission signal – it is still registering that the microchip is working and coming from the area you are watching.

Suddenly, a thought strikes you... "What if the chip has been found? What if the werewolf has—"

"Looking for me?"

You feel a tap on the shoulder and spin around. It's the waitress werewolf – and she's got a knife. Before you can reach for your gun, the creature has the knife at your throat.

"You shouldn't have let me live! The microchip is in the pool with the polar bears. Not a very nice thing to inject into my body. But Lykon guessed you would have done something like this. It was just a matter of waiting for you. The Hunter has been hunted down... Lykon wishes to meet you. I don't know why – I think you should die, so don't do anything stupid, or else." The creature moves the knife from your throat and points it at your side. "You will come with me, but not as you are..." And then, before your eyes, she begins to transform into wolf form.

‡ *If you decide to do as the werewolf says, go to 86.*
‡ *If you wish to use your martial arts skills, go to 28.*
‡ *If you wish to reach for a weapon, go to 23.*

# 98

"Go and check it out, while I finish loading up the snowmobile," you tell Bradfield and the guards. "Then let me know what you find."

Bradfield and the guards nod agreement and head towards the store.

You continue to load your weapons onto the snowmobile's sled. You are nearly finished when you hear yells and shouts ringing out across the compound. You glance up to see what the noise is all about and your heart misses a beat.

Standing before you is a creature from your worst nightmares. It is a cross between a human and a wolf.

97: The werewolf waitress begins to transform.

Its body is horribly mutilated and it stands on its hind legs, but it has human arms and hands, not paws. Its wolf-like face has chunks of flesh and fur missing and the creature's internal organs hang from gaping wounds in its hairy torso.

You scramble for your gun, but you are too slow. The werewolf swipes at you, knocking you out. You fall to the ground, unconscious.

‡ *Go to 6.*

## 99

You spin across the floor at speed, grab hold of the chainsaw and leap up, holding the blade out. As you try to start it, the werewolf pounces.

You curse and realise that you can't start the chainsaw. You try to use it as a lance, holding it out to fend off your attacker, but the werewolf swats the saw from your grip and moves in for the kill.

You lash out at the beast, but your martial arts skills are of no use against this supernatural creature. It soon overpowers you and clamps its great jaws around on your neck, snapping it like a twig.

‡ *You have failed to defeat the werewolves. If you wish to try again, go to 1.*

**99:** The werewolf moves in for the kill.

# 100

Lykon leaps at you with his great jaws apart, but as he does you use your martial arts skills to throw him off to one side. You jump to your feet and pull the pin on the grenade. Lykon pounces at you again. With one twisting movement you thrust the grenade into the werewolf's mouth and sweep his legs out from under him, sending Lykon flying over the edge.

Lykon plunges downwards through the night sky, howling in anger and surprise before its howls are cut off as the grenade explodes inside the werewolf's body, the silver shards lighting up the sky like a firework.

The helicopters with their news crews buzz around capturing every last shot as you stand on the crown, victorious.

"And that's what will happen to any of you creatures that have any thoughts of messing with humankind," you shout out.

As the remains of the werewolf float down onto the black waters below, you wave at the helicopters. "Can I hitch a lift with any of you guys? I need to get home and have a rest."

But deep inside, you know that there are many more challenges for you if you are to keep humanity safe from the creatures of the dark.

# About the 2Steves

Steve Barlow and Steve Skidmore have been writing together for over twenty years. Known as the 2Steves, they have written over 125 books together.

**Visit www.the2steves.net**

### Steve Barlow

- ✣ Born: Crewe, UK
- ✣ Description: Tall and hairy
- ✣ Most horrific job: Emptying rubbish bins
- ✣ Most horrific pet: Igor the cannibal gerbil
- ✣ Favourite horror creature: Mothra – I just love the idea of a gigantic moth that destroys whole cities!
- ✣ Favourite horror film: *An American Werewolf in London*

### Steve Skidmore

- ✣ Born: Leicester, UK
- ✣ Description: Short and less hairy than Barlow
- ✣ Most horrific job: Counting pastry pie lids
- ✣ Most horrific pet: A mad rabbit
- ✣ Favourite horror creature: Vampire
- ✣ Favourite horror film: *The Omen*

Steve Barlow

Steve Skidmore

# iHorror: werewolf facts

Werewolves, also called "lycanthropes", appeared in books written by the Greeks and Romans, and in legends told during the Middle Ages across Europe. Many tales have things in common, but not all of them are accurate.

**True facts about werewolves:**

‡ They don't always need a full moon to shapeshift. When the moon is full, a werewolf is at full strength though.

‡ A werewolf is created if you are born a werewolf, bitten by one, or if you become cursed. You cannot remove the curse – ever.

‡ It is now known that werewolves can be killed by silver entering their heart – usually a blade made of pure silver (watch out for fakes) or solid silver bullets.

**Common mistakes include:**

‡ Trying to use a crucifix to scare off a werewolf won't work.

‡ Drinking from the footprint of a werewolf won't turn you into one.

**Bet you didn't know:**

The first film to feature a werewolf was a silent feature called *The Werewolf* made in 1913.

# Creating the artwork of iHorror

*The inside artwork for iHorror is drawn by Paul Davidson. We've put together some pieces to show you the stages of progression. Below is the scene from paragraph 12, when Lykon starts the Great Hunt. Paul says: "Here the rough pencil and ink final have been merged along side each other. At the rough stage I'm really only looking to capture the positions and content – the fur details and blocking out can come later."*

"Here you can see how messy and confusing a rough can get, especially when there are different elements in the foreground and background. The inking process in the final gives the piece more depth and clarity."

"This is one of the editor's favourite pieces. The texture of Lykon's beard and coat changes from the rough to the final."

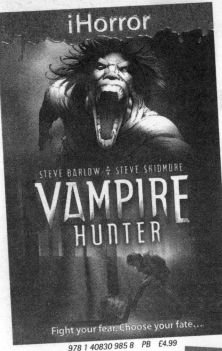

# iHorror

## Win a Nintendo DS Lite!*

### The hunt is on...

Prove your skill as a hunter by locating the
Hunter silhouettes lurking in the pages of the
iHorror books (your first one is at the bottom
of this page). Once you have found them in ALL
FOUR iHorror titles, write the TOTAL number of
silhouettes on a postcard with your name, age
and address, and send it to:

iHorror Hunter Competition
Orchard Books Marketing Department
338 Euston Road
London NW1 3BH

Or email your answer and details to:
competitions@hachettechildrens.co.uk

Competition closes 31 August 2011.

For full terms and conditions visit:
www.orchardbooks.co.uk

*Fight your fear. Choose your fate.*

*This competition will run across all four iHorror books published
in 2011. There will be one prize draw. Only one entry per child.